Tara stepped over rolls of old carpet, ducking under cobwebs with their sleepy spiders.

At-choo! The dust made her sneeze, and then she reached what she was looking for. The old wooden costume box!

She knelt down in front of it and reached towards the metal clasp. She felt a rush of excitement, knowing that once again, something amazing was about to happen.

3

The box was full of outfits of all shapes and sizes. There were uniforms, helmets, overalls, jackets, boots … there was a costume for every job Tara could think of. But, for Tara, the box had more than just costumes. It was full of big ideas, and it always put Tara in an outfit that she wouldn't normally have chosen for herself.

She pushed up the heavy wooden lid. As she did so, a tingling started in her fingertips, and flowed through her hands and right up her arms. She grinned because she knew what was going to happen next.

Swirling mist surrounded her, and Tara just had time to wonder, *What will I be today?* before she felt herself tumbling through space and time, whisked away on another exciting adventure.

Tara Binns

Trail-blazing Astronaut

Written by Lisa Rajan

Illustrated by Alessia Trunfio

Collins

Chapter 1

Tara Binns pushed open the loft hatch door and poked her head into the dim and dusty attic room. Scrambling up the last steps of the ladder, she crawled through the small opening on to the wooden floorboards.

Tara stood up, brushing the grey dust off her knees. Now ... where was it? She surveyed the untidy space under the rafters at the top of her house. Ah! Over there!

Chapter 2

When Tara opened her eyes again, she was looking down at
the craters of the Moon. They looked so close. She gasped,
and realised she was floating in front of a small,
round window. Her feet weren't touching anything.

Am I in a spaceship? she wondered.

Tara looked down at herself. She was wearing bright yellow overalls with a zip up the front. There was a patch on her right shoulder showing an owl flying over a lunar landscape. It said **Minerva Mission**. Tara spied the same patch on the yellow overalls of the girl floating next to her.

"I'm an astronaut!" Tara exclaimed.

"You certainly are," agreed the girl. "You're on the Minerva-7, orbiting the Moon. I'm Commander Ayesha, and I'm promoting you to Flight Engineer. We're going down to the Moon's surface to rescue Mission Specialist Ortez. And we've got to do it fast!"

Tara's eyes nearly popped out of her head. It was one thing to be in space, but actually to walk on the Moon? And to rescue someone! Wow!

"What happened to Ortez?" she asked.

"He was just on a normal mission. He's done loads of them. He took one of Minerva's three lunar landers down to the Moon's surface yesterday – the Luna-1. He was collecting rock samples. He tests them to see if they have special properties that are different from the rocks on Earth. If they are strong enough, we could use them to build a settlement on the Moon."

Tara's head was reeling. She couldn't take it all in.

Ayesha continued: "Houses, roads, tunnels … who knows what might be possible."

Tara faltered. "B-but Ortez? Is he OK?"

"We don't know …" Ayesha replied gravely. "Ortez was analysing some of his samples when something bad happened."

Ayesha went on: "A meteorite storm struck, and it was much bigger than we were expecting!" Her eyes widened. "Terrifying – hundreds of rocks, pelting the surface of the Moon. Some of them bigger than footballs! Big enough to make new craters –"

"And Ortez?" asked Tara.

"Luckily, he wasn't outside when the storm struck. He was in the Luna-1. But that *did* get hit. He says it's badly damaged and he can't take off to return to the Minerva. So we need to get him back before the next storm hits. There's another one expected in the next few hours, but it's tricky to be sure when it will arrive."

Ayesha pointed at two bulky white spacesuits.

"Put on one of these. We'll take the second lunar lander, the Luna-2, and we'll head down on our next orbit around the Moon."

Ayesha typed numbers into the onboard computer. She was working out the exact moment the Luna-2 needed to separate from the Command Ship Minerva-7. Then the Moon's gravity would take the lunar lander gracefully down to where Ortez was stuck.

Chapter 3

Tara and Ayesha pulled through the airlock into the Luna-2. It was smaller than Tara was expecting. The control panel looked complicated – four small screens and lots of dials, buttons and switches. They were in zero-gravity and the walls were covered with metal cases that clipped into place to stop them moving about during the flight.

The rest of the inside looked very basic – lots of pipes and wires, and three seats. Tara sat down on one of them.

"Strap yourself in," said Ayesha, looking at one of the screens. "The blasters will separate us from the command ship in ten seconds. Ten … nine … eight … seven…"

Tara buckled her safety belt. She gripped the side of her seat, nervously.

"Three … two … one …"

WHOOOSH!

It was a smooth separation – not the jolt Tara had been expecting. The jolt came 24 seconds later, when …

BANG!

Something hit the Luna-2, sending it into a stomach-lurching spin.

"What was *that*?" Tara cried, her heart racing.
The spinning was making her feel sick.

"I don't know," said Ayesha, looking at the computer
screens. "Maybe the next meteorite storm has come early."

Tara looked over at Ayesha. She was frowning with
concentration and flicking several switches. Each one
fired a blast of compressed air in the opposite direction
to the one they were spinning in. This slowed the spin
down until, at last, it stopped and they glided gently down
towards the Moon.

Tara's heart was still thumping when she saw Ayesha staring at the screens again. Then Ayesha started typing on the keyboard at lightning speed.

"What's wrong?" Tara asked, with dread in her voice.

"The meteorite knocked us off course. I calculate we'll land about a kilometre beyond where Ortez is. And that will be a disaster."

"What can we do?" asked Tara.

"I'll have to use the blasters again. But I'll have to time it … just … right …" said Ayesha. "We'll come down very fast. And I won't be able to control the landing, so we'll crash. Brace yourself, Tara!"

Tara gripped her seat again. She squeezed her eyes shut and held her breath.

She heard Ayesha count them down to landing:

"… three … two … one …"

CRASH!

There was a huge jolt, followed by a shudder.

Tara opened her eyes and looked around. They seemed to be in one piece. She breathed out … *Phew!*

Ayesha was checking the control panel again. Something was flashing red on the screen.

"What's wrong now?" asked Tara, her relief turning to fear.

"That landing damaged the third blaster. Put your helmet on. We need to go outside to take a look."

Tara gulped. She was about to walk on the Moon!

Chapter 4

Everything was eerily quiet and still as Tara climbed
down the ladder and took her first step on to the Moon.
She looked around her. Against the inky blackness of space
and the pinpricks of a million distant stars, the grey craters
of the lunar landscape looked stunning. Planet Earth was
rising over the horizon. It took her breath away.

"Amazing, isn't it?" said Ayesha, over the radio in
their helmets. "Like nothing on Earth!"

Tara nodded, speechless in wonder at it all. She looked
at the footprints she had made in the dust.

"They'll be there forever," said Ayesha, seriously.
"There's no wind or rain to destroy them here."

Ayesha walked around the Luna-2's spider-like frame.
Each step was more of a slow bounce in the Moon's
low gravity. It was like walking along the bottom of
a swimming pool. She spotted the damaged blaster.

"Bad news, Flight Engineer Binns," she said quietly. "It's
completely buckled. The jets are broken. So are the fixings
attaching the blaster to the lunar lander's leg. We can't take
off again. We're stuck."

Tara's heart dropped like a stone. What a nightmare!

"Unless –" began Ayesha.

"Unless what?" asked Tara, hopefully.

"Unless Ortez can help us ..." said Ayesha, nodding towards an astronaut climbing out of a crater.

Ortez spotted them and waved. He pointed to the Luna-1 and beckoned them to follow. Soon they were climbing into the Luna-1. Panting a little, they went through the airlock and took off their helmets. Ortez was carrying a bag of moondust. He put it down on one of the seats.

"Am I glad to see you!" said Ortez. "I'll get the rest of my samples and we'll get out of here before the next meteorite storm hits. Can you grab those bottles, please? I need them to test this strange moondust I found. But I'll do that once we're on our way!"

"Bad news, I'm afraid," said Ayesha slowly. "The Luna-2 got hit by a meteorite on the way here and we had to crash land. The third blaster was damaged. It won't work. You're still stuck … and now we are too."

Ortez looked shocked. "Can I have a look?"

They put their helmets back on, grabbed the toolkit and headed outside. Ortez surveyed the damage. He shook his head. The blaster really was smashed. There was no way now to get enough thrust to power back up into orbit. And without that blaster, they couldn't steer properly, either. Ortez and Ayesha looked at each other. No one spoke.

Tara looked at the Luna-1 and then at the Luna-2. Two lunar landers, but neither could get off the ground.

If only we could combine the working bits of both, she thought.

Hmmm … Maybe we could!

"Ayesha! Ortez!" she shouted. "Maybe this is a crazy idea, but could we put the working blaster from the Luna-1 on to the Luna-2?"

Ayesha thought for a few moments.

"Yes … it might work," she said.

"Let's look," said Ortez, examining the fixings. But then he pulled a face and shook his head.

"We could get a working blaster off the Luna-1 … but the fixings on the Luna-2 have buckled. We can't attach anything to them."

"So, we're stuck here?" asked Tara, feeling scared.

"We'll have to radio the Minerva and get them to send the third lunar lander down to rescue us," said Ayesha.

"Phew!" Tara breathed a sigh of relief. "So we'll be all right!"

"We should be … as long as –" started Ayesha.

"As long as what?" demanded Tara.

"As long as we don't run out of air while we're waiting for them."

Chapter 5

They climbed back into the Luna-1. Ortez radioed up to the command ship.

"Come in, Minerva-7 … this is Luna-1. The Luna-2 is damaged. Can you please send down the Luna-3?"

"Negative, Luna-1. There's a problem with the Luna-3. A power surge has blown the electrics. The engineers are working on it, but it's pretty bad. We'll know more in a few hours."

The blood drained out of Tara's face. She felt faint. The Luna-3 had been their last hope. She shunted the bag of moondust off the seat and sat down just before her legs gave way. The bag split as it hit the floor, spilling dust all around Tara's boots.

"We don't have a few hours, Minerva-7. We're running out of air," said Ayesha calmly.

"I'm afraid you don't have a few hours, anyway," came the voice of Ayesha's Second-in-Command. "There's more bad news ..."

More bad news! thought Tara. She felt sick. Ayesha and Ortez looked at each other.

The Second-in-Command continued: "… there's another meteorite storm on its way. It's heading straight for you. Most of the rocks will hit in an hour or so, but a few strays may reach you much sooner than that. You have to find a way to get off the Moon … and quickly."

Tara gasped. She flashed a panicked look at Ortez and Ayesha, but they seemed calm and quiet. Both were thinking hard.

I must get a grip, thought Tara.

SMASH!

The noise was deafening. The Luna-1 shuddered with the impact. The rack of chemicals from the moondust analysis kit wobbled and fell over.

BANG!

Tara clapped her hands over her ears.

"What was that?" she shouted.

"I think it was one of those stray meteorites," said Ortez.

"No, not tha—"

"We need to get out of here," interrupted Ayesha, putting on her helmet. "Let's have another look at that blaster. There must be something we can do ..."

Ortez followed her towards the door. Tara rose to follow them. But as she stepped over the spilt moondust, she noticed that the chemicals from the analysis kit were mixing with it.

And something very strange was happening …

Chapter 6

Tara bent down to take a closer look. Something was happening to the moondust where the chemicals had landed on it. The mixture was fizzing and flowing in a gloopy purple stream across the metal floor.

"Come on, Tara!" cried Ortez over his shoulder.

But Tara couldn't take her eyes off the bubbling mixture. Then something even stranger happened. After a few seconds, the mixture seemed to harden and become shiny and still. Tara reached out and touched it carefully with her gloved hand. It had gone solid! It was as hard as a rock and had stuck fast to the metal floor.

"Ortez," called Tara. "Look at this –"

"Leave that mess!" said Ortez, impatiently. "It's the least
of our problems! We need to find a way to attach the working
blaster to the Luna-2 –"

"I know," said Tara, with a glimmer of excitement in
her voice. "And I think I might have just found one!"

Something in Tara's voice made Ortez stop, and he came and knelt down to have a look. He saw the moondust mixture bubble and ooze, before turning solid a few seconds later. He grabbed a screwdriver from his toolkit and stabbed as hard as he could at the dark shiny blob. It didn't even scratch.

"Ayesha!" he called out, excitedly. "I think Tara's right!"

Ayesha pulled off her helmet. She looked angry.

"What are you up to?"

Ortez began to explain.

"This moondust mixture is making some sort of gooey paste –"

"Like glue!" interrupted Tara.

"… which sets when it comes into contact with metal," went on Ortez.

"Like concrete!" cried Tara.

Ayesha's jaw dropped.

"I see what you're saying! You think we could use it to *stick* the blaster from the Luna-1 on to the Luna-2!"

Tara grinned.

"Can we give it a try?"

"We'll have to use exactly the same ingredients," said Ortez, reading the label on the empty bottle. "I hope there's more of this."

"At least there's plenty of moondust!" said Tara.

"That's not ordinary moondust," said Ortez. "It came from the bottom of a really deep crater made by a meteorite. That dust was much darker than normal. I thought it might be special, but I never guessed at this!"

Very carefully, Ayesha took off the broken blaster from the Luna-2. Then Tara helped her hold the working blaster from the Luna-1 in position.

Ortez poured the chemicals into a jar of dark moondust. Nothing happened. He shook the mixture around. Still nothing. What was wrong? Why wasn't it fizzing and bubbling?

"Was there another ingredient, Tara? We must have forgotten something."

Tara puffed out her cheeks as she thought hard. Had there been something else in the mix? She breathed out sharply.

Of course! That was it!

"Air!" cried Tara. "There was air inside the Luna-1! Maybe the oxygen in air sets the chemical reaction going ..."

Ayesha bounced up the ladder to the Luna-2 and came back with their last air tank.

"I hope this works," she said quietly. "We don't have any more."

She attached the hose from the air tank to the moondust mixture.

Fizzz ... *bubble* ... It was working!

It was tricky pouring the thick glue between the fixings and the blaster. But after several messy goes, they did it and the glue set rock hard. The blaster was stuck as firmly as if it had been welded on.

Whizzz … THUD! A small rock the size of a ping-pong ball flew past Tara's helmet.

THUD! And another one.

THUD … THUD … THUD! They were coming like hailstones now.

"Quick, get inside the Luna-2!" shouted Ayesha. Ortez and Tara did not need to be told twice.

Chapter 7

They raced inside the Luna-2.

"This meteorite storm had better stop soon," said Ortez. "We need to take off in exactly four minutes, if we're going to dock with the Minerva. Otherwise we won't catch them on this orbit."

Tara looked blank.

Ortez explained, "The Minerva-7 has been circling the Moon the whole time we've been down here. We're going to blast off and aim to reach the Minerva's orbit at the exact moment it comes around. Then we can dock with it."

Ortez drew Tara a picture to show what he meant.

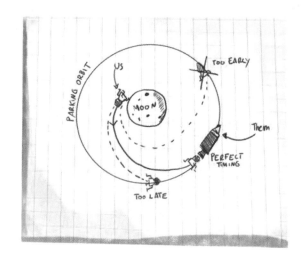

He warned, "If we take off too late or too early, we'll end up too far behind the Minerva or too far in front, but not close enough to dock with it."

Ayesha and Ortez got ready to take off as soon as the meteorite storm stopped. Tara kept watch out of the window. But the meteorites kept coming.

One minute passed.

"Can't we just take our chances?" asked Tara. "These meteorites aren't very big."

"They'll still knock us off course. And we don't know if the blaster we replaced will hold. We *can't* chance it – we could be drifting in space forever."

Three minutes passed.

Then the clock ticked down to zero.

Ortez shook his head. They'd missed their time slot. They were too late to dock with the Minerva-7 on this orbit. Ortez slumped in his seat. For the first time, he looked defeated.

"How long until the Minerva comes around again?" asked Tara.

"Two hours," replied Ayesha.

"Do we have enough air to wait for it?" asked Tara, hopefully.

"No," said Ayesha. "We have about 30 minutes of air left. We used up the spare air tank making the glue, remember?"

"There *must* be something we can do ..." Tara said in a small voice.

No one replied. Ortez shrugged. Ayesha put her head in her hands. The only sounds were the light thuds of the last few meteorites hitting the Luna-2. The storm was almost over.

Tara stared blankly at Ortez's sketch. She felt desperate. Her eyes followed the arrow leading the Luna-2 up to the meeting point with the command ship.

Hang on … what had Ortez said?

The Minerva-7 has been circling the Moon … We blast off … reach their orbit … dock with them …

What if …? Could we …?

Tara had a glimmer of an idea that just might work.

She grabbed the sketch, tracing their take-off with her finger. Then she stopped and traced it in the *opposite* direction.

"Ortez! What if we went the other way? Instead of travelling in the same direction as the Minerva-7, we could meet it coming the other way – head on!"

She drew a line on Ortez's sketch to show them what she meant. Ortez's eyes widened.

"I suppose … yes … it could work!"

"Let me work out how we should take off ..." said Ayesha.

She typed furiously on the computer keyboard, pausing only to check Tara's sketch and to do a few calculations in her head.

Ortez radioed the command ship.

"Come in, Minerva-7! This is Luna-2. We missed our take-off window because of the meteorite storm, but we're going to head around to meet you the other way. You'll have to slow right down as we get close. We estimate we'll meet you in –"

He looked up at Ayesha.

"22 minutes," she said, "which means we'll need to take off in three minutes."

Can we do it? wondered Tara.

She crossed her fingers.

Chapter 8

Tara stared out of the small round window at the lunar landscape. All was quiet and still.

"The storm is over. We're clear to go!" she called to Ortez and Ayesha.

Ortez rechecked the dials and screens, preparing the Luna-2 for take-off.

"Three … two … one …" Ayesha fired the three blasters. Each one shot out a jet of air, lifting them up from the Moon's surface. She then turned two of the blasters off, to change direction. The turn was smooth … no rattles, no wobbles … the glue on the third blaster was holding!

They continued rising up and up, away from the still beauty of the lunar landscape. Tara couldn't take her eyes off it. It was strange to think that she'd left her footprints in the dust there forever.

They reached the orbit of the Minerva-7. Tara could see it approaching. Both spacecraft slowed down.

"Docking will be tricky ..." said Ayesha. "Tara, can you help me line up with the Minerva? I'll control the first two rocket blasters, you take the third. It has to be perfect –"

BEEP! BEEP! BEEP! BEEP!

The alarm made Tara jump. Her eyes shot to the light flashing on the control panel.

AIR SUPPLY LOW.

Tara gulped, then focused again. Ayesha eased the Luna-2 to the left … then to the right …

"One last blast, Flight Engineer Binns!" she commanded.

PFFFTT!

CLANG!

The two spacecraft made contact. Tara clung to the sides of her seat. Everything wobbled … and then was still.

"Come in, Luna-2! This is the Minerva-7. Docking successful! Welcome back! The airlock is open – come on through!"

Tara undid her seatbelt and pushed up out of her seat. *Woah!* She felt light-headed. Had they run out of air, or had she just got up too quickly?

She felt Ortez pulling her towards the airlock.
He reached for the handle and yanked the door open. Air!
They were safe!

"We made it!" Tara cheered. "You did it, Ayesha!"

"It wasn't just me," smiled Ayesha, raising her hand for
a high five. "We're a team. And it was your great idea to
go the other way that got us back here before we ran out
of air."

"And don't forget," Ortez added, pointing to the blaster,
"without you, we'd be missing the glue that keeps us
all together!"

Tara clapped her hand against Ayesha's, grinning
with pride.

Suddenly, Tara felt her hand tingling … then the tingling spread up her arm.

The spaceship began spinning … or was it her? It was hard to tell when you were already in zero-gravity. She was surrounded by a whirling, swirling mist and then suddenly, Tara felt herself tumbling in time as well as space until …

KA-BOOM!

Chapter 9

The next moment, Tara was back in the attic. The whirling and swirling stopped and the mist cleared. Tara looked down at the dusty floorboards. It was good to have something solid beneath her feet again.

She removed the helmet and took a deep breath of the still dusty air. It tasted so different back down on Earth. She grinned to herself.

Being an astronaut was amazing – truly out of this world! I took small steps on the Moon and a giant leap off it!

Tara took the spacesuit off and placed it carefully back inside the box.

Perhaps I'll be an astronaut when I grow up, she thought, her eyes twinkling. *I'll reach for the stars and boldly go wherever my dreams take me. A galaxy far, far away or a lopsided lunar landing … Whatever it is, it'll be a blast!*

Being an astronaut

bravery

adventurousness

imagination

curiosity

problem solving

teamwork

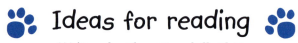

Ideas for reading

Written by Clare Dowdall, PhD
Lecturer and Primary Literacy Consultant

Reading objectives:
- explore the meaning of words in context
- draw inferences such as inferring characters' feelings, thoughts and motives from their actions, and justify inferences with evidence
- predict what might happen from details stated and implied
- summarise the main ideas drawn from more than one paragraph, identifying key details that support the main ideas

Spoken language objectives:
- use spoken language to develop understanding through speculating, hypothesising, imagining and exploring ideas
- participate in discussions, presentations, performances, role play, improvisations and debates

Curriculum links: Science – Earth and space

Interest words: lunar landscape, astronaut, settlement, meteorite storm, zero-gravity, compressed, chemicals, orbit, docking

Resources: paper, pens and pencils, sticky notes, computer/tablet for research

Build a context for reading

- Read the title and blurb. Discuss what children know about the work of an astronaut.
- Read through the interest words together and explain the meaning of any unknown words.
- Ask children to make a list of the qualities Tara might need to be a successful astronaut.

Understand and apply reading strategies

- Ask for a volunteer to read pp2–4 aloud. Help children to relate to Tara's situation by asking them what they would like to become if they were using the costume box, and why.
- Read pp6–11 together. Ask children to recount what has happened to Tara as precisely as possible, referring to the facts in the story.